creatures of the sea

Flying Fish

Other titles in the series:

Beluga Whales

The Crab

Dolphins

Humpback Whales

Jellyfish

Lobsters

Moray Eels

The Octopus

Rays

Sea Horses

Sea Stars

Squid

The Walrus

The Whale Shark

creatures of the sea

Flying Fish

Kris Hirschmann

KIDHAVEN PRESS
An imprint of Thomson Gale, a part of The Thomson Corporation

THOMSON
GALE ™

Detroit • New York • San Francisco • San Diego • New Haven, Conn.
Waterville, Maine • London • Munich

THOMSON
GALE

For more information, contact
KidHaven Press
27500 Drake Rd.
Farmington Hills, MI 48331-3535
Or you can visit our Internet site at http://www.gale.com

LIBRARY OF CONGRESS CATALOGING-IN-PUBLICATION DATA

Hirschmann, Kris, 1967–
Flying Fish / by Kris Hirschmann.
p. cm.—(Creatures of the sea)
Summary: Discusses the habitat, anatomy, reproductive cycle, and predators of flying fish.
Includes bibliographical references and index.
ISBN 0-7377-2341-6 (hardcover: alk. paper)
1. Flying fish—Juvenile literature. I. Title.
QL638 .E9H57 2004
597'66—dc22

2004013529

Printed in the United States of America

Table of Contents

Introduction

Flights of Fancy

A boat cuts through sparkling, sun-kissed seas, bouncing gently as waves break against its prow. The ocean is calm and quiet all around. Then suddenly the surface is broken as a small fish hurls itself out of the water and away from the approaching boat. The fish zips through the air with a buzzing sound. After traveling what seems an incredible distance, the creature finally drops back into the sea with a small splash and disappears from view. The flying fish has returned to its ocean home.

This scene is repeated over and over in tropical waters around the world. Flying fish are very common, and so are their amazing flights. Because these animals are among the few sea creatures that regularly leave the water, they are among the

A group of four-winged flying fish skims the surface of the open ocean.

world's best-known fish. Anyone who travels through warm seas is bound to catch a glimpse of these incredible animals.

Flying fish may be common, but they are thrilling nonetheless. A fish on the wing seems to challenge the very laws of nature. Perhaps for this reason, flying fish have captured the imagination of many writers and poets. In his poem "Mandalay," for example, author Rudyard Kipling refers to "the road to Mandalay, where the flyin'-fishes play." Author Ernest Hemingway also mentions flying fish in his book *The Old Man and the Sea*. The book's main character, Santiago, hears "the trembling sound as flying fish left the water and the hissing that their stiff wings made as they soared away in the darkness." And in his book *Following the Equator*, author Mark Twain describes a tall tale–telling Scot who "told about a pet flying-fish he once owned, that lived in a little fountain in his conservatory, and supported itself by catching birds and frogs and rats in the neighboring fields."

It is not surprising that flying fish appear in books and poems. Although these animals are just fish, their ability to soar through the air makes them seem exotic and special. Today, as in ages past, the sight of a flying fish skipping over the waves is something that will not soon be forgotten.

Chapter 1

Dragonflies of the Sea

When people want to describe something that just does not seem right, they sometimes use the phrase "a fish out of water." This phrase suggests that a fish is in the wrong place any time it leaves its watery home. For most fish, this is true. But one type of fish is at home both below *and* above the ocean surface. This animal is called the flying fish.

There are more than fifty species of flying fish. All flying fish are included in the scientific family **Exocoetidae**. This name comes from the Greek words *exo*, meaning "outside," and *koite*, meaning "nest" or "hollow." It refers to the flying fish's habit of leaving its ocean home or "nest" by launching itself into the air. Because of this amazing ability, flying fish have also earned the nickname "dragonflies of the sea."

Where Flying Fish Live

Flying fish are saltwater creatures. They are extremely common throughout the Atlantic, Pacific, and Indian oceans. They can also be found in the Red Sea, the Mediterranean, the Gulf of Mexico, and other large saltwater bodies. Especially big groups gather around isolated islands, since these out-of-the-way places make excellent breeding grounds. However, islands are not the only place to see flying fish. These animals live everywhere from the coastal waters near continents to the remote waters of the open sea. Some species have a strong preference for one type of habitat. The African flying fish, for example, is found only in open waters, and the backspot flying fish lives only in coastal areas. Other species, such as the margined flying fish and the **four-winged flying fish**, can be found in both coastal and open-sea areas. And some species migrate from one region to another at different times of the year.

Most flying fish species are tropical, living in the warm waters near the earth's equator. Common tropical species include the **two-winged flying fish** and the sailfin flying fish. A few species can tolerate a wider range of temperatures and can be found in cooler seas. The Atlantic flying fish, for example,

A flying fish struggles on a fisherman's line off the coast of Barbados in the Caribbean Sea.

may live as far north as Canada. The mirrorwing flying fish swims in the chilly waters off the coast of New Zealand, and the spotfin flying fish may be seen in seas anywhere from the northern United States to the southern tip of South America.

Wherever they are found, all flying fish have one habit in common. They stick to the extreme upper regions of the ocean. Every now and then a flying fish may dive as far as 60 feet (18.3 meters) below the water's surface when looking for food, but these deep dives do not last long. After finding what it wants, the fish quickly pops back up to the sea surface.

The Flying Fish Body

All flying fish share certain physical features. These animals' bodies are nearly round, not flattened from side to side or top to bottom like the bodies of many fish. The trunk is covered with large, soft scales that protect the fish's delicate skin. Scales also streamline the flying fish's body to let it cut more easily through the water. The flying fish's jaws are very short and almost equal in length, and the spine is unusually bony and rigid. A strong spine is important because it helps to support the body's weight when the flying fish leaves the water.

Despite these similarities, it is fairly easy to tell one flying fish species from another. Different types of flying fish have different features that help to set them apart. The most obvious difference is size. The largest species is the California flying fish, which can grow to about eighteen inches (forty-six centimeters) in length. The smallest species, the African sailfin flying fish, reaches a maximum length of only four inches (ten centimeters). All other types of flying fish fall somewhere between these extremes. Most species measure about eight to twelve inches (twenty to thirty centimeters) from tip to tip.

Coloration is another difference between species. Flying fish may bear spots, stripes, and other unique markings, especially on their **pectoral fins**. Species' common names often refer to these markings. The

The California flying fish is the largest species, sometimes reaching eighteen inches in length.

manyspotted flying fish, for example, has light blue pectoral fins sprinkled with small dark spots. The pectoral fins of the yellowband flying fish are lined with yellowish white bands.

Amazing Fins

The pectoral fins of the flying fish are important for more than just identification. They also act as wings, allowing the flying fish to soar gracefully through the air. The pectoral fins are found just behind the fish's head and are attached toward the top of the body. In the water, the pectoral fins are closed and held tightly

The wings of the flying fish are actually fins that allow the fish to soar after leaving the water.

A woman in Barbados holds a flying fish she has caught by its pectoral fins.

against the flying fish's sides. Out of the water, they can be spread into large, rigid wings. The flying fish opens these wings by spreading stiff rays within the pectoral fins. The rays act like the spokes of an umbrella to support the delicate skin in between.

Anatomy of a Flying Fish

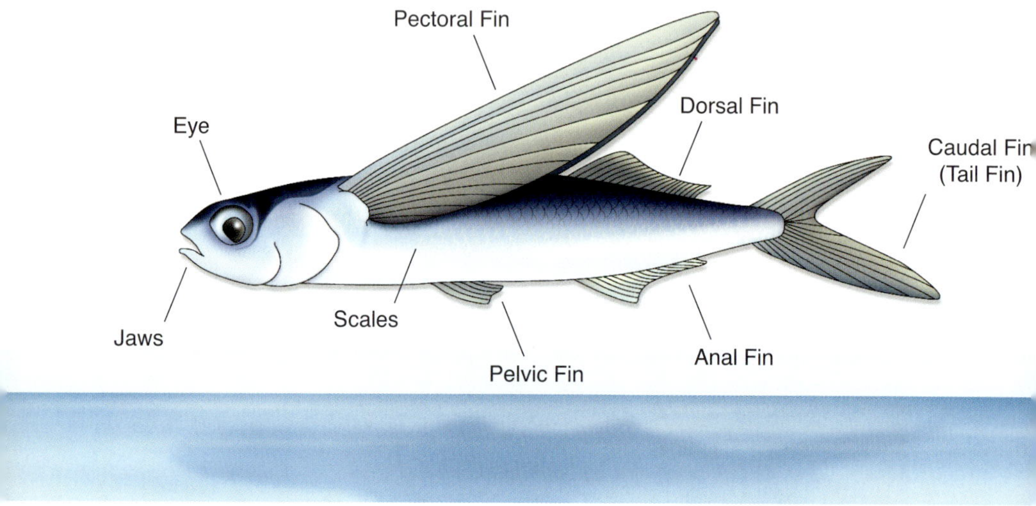

Farther back on the body are two **pelvic fins**. The pelvic fins are attached to the sides, near the bottom of the fish's trunk. In most species of flying fish, the pelvic fins are small and delicate. In a few species, however, the pelvic fins are large and sturdy. Out of the water, they can be spread just like the pectoral fins. Big pelvic fins look and act like a second pair of wings, so species with this feature are called four-winged flying fish. Species with small pelvic fins are called two-winged flying fish.

Behind the pelvic fins are the **dorsal** and **anal fins**. The dorsal fin stands up from the fish's back, and the anal fin sticks down from the belly. Both fins help to stabilize the flying fish as it moves through the water. Like the pectoral and pelvic fins, the dorsal and anal fins are supported by stiff rays. The flying fish can move these rays to change the size, shape, and angle of the fins. By doing this, the fish changes its direction in the same way a sailor changes a boat's direction by moving the rudder from side to side.

At the rear of the flying fish's body is a large tail fin, also called the **caudal fin**. All flying fish have deeply forked tails, with the bottom lobe being much larger than the top lobe. The flying fish uses strong muscles in its tail to wave its caudal fin back and forth. This motion creates a push that moves the fish forward through the water.

Sensing the World

Like all fish, the flying fish depends on its senses for information about the world. Vision is this animal's most important sense. All flying fish have big eyes in relation to their bodies. Large eyes gather lots of light, which makes them very sensitive even at night. Good night vision is essential for an animal that is always on the lookout for predators.

The position of the flying fish's eyes is also important. The eyes look out to both sides of the flying fish's body instead of forward. Because of this positioning, a flying fish cannot focus well on objects. Forward-looking eyes are better for accurate vision. However, the flying fish has a much wider range of vision than a forward-looking animal does.

A wide range of vision lets flying fish see enemies approaching from the sides, not just the front. This advance warning helps flying fish to react quickly in dangerous situations.

The flying fish's eyes have one last interesting feature. They are specially adapted to work both in and out of the water. This ability is important for an animal that regularly launches itself out of the sea. A flying fish can see where it is going after it leaves the water. Once it is in the air, the fish can watch for hungry seabirds attacking from above, and it

The eyes of the flying fish are adapted to work well both in and out of the water.

may even be able to look for predators in the water below. If a flying fish spots danger in the air, it can dive back into the ocean. If it sees danger in the water, it can keep soaring or change its direction to avoid being caught and eaten. In this way, vision helps the flying fish to stay alive.

Although vision is the flying fish's most important sense, it is not the only sense at work. Smell, hearing, and touch also give these creatures information about their underwater homes. Between all these senses, flying fish have all the input they need to survive in the ocean world.

chapter 2

Life as a Flying Fish

Flying fish do not have long lives. Some may reach one to two years of age. Most, however, do not live nearly this long. A large percentage of flying fish are eaten by predators soon after they hatch, and many others will become meals for other animals when they are adults.

Still, there are plenty of flying fish in the seas. Female flying fish lay enormous numbers of eggs during their lifetimes. Each of these eggs contains a flying fish **embryo**. If just a few of these embryos reach adulthood, the flying fish population will remain strong and healthy.

Spawning Grounds and Cycles

Flying fish of all species live together in schools. These schools may shift from place to place at different times of the year. Many species, for example, spend most of their lives far out at sea. But when it is time to **spawn** (release eggs and sperm into the water), these creatures flock to special breeding grounds near land. The Coromandel flying fish is one species that follows this pattern. These creatures swim the open waters of the Indian Ocean during the fall, winter, and spring months. Between June and September, however, they are found in huge numbers off the coast of Sri Lanka. The sailfin flying fish is another species that sometimes comes near land when it is time to spawn. In 2001 scientists spotted a breeding group of these animals

in the Gulf of Mexico about sixty miles (one hundred kilometers) south of Mobile, Alabama. An estimated 1 million flying fish participated in this spawning frenzy.

The Sargasso Sea, a 2-million-square-mile (5.2-million-square-kilometer) mat of seaweed in the central North Atlantic Ocean, is an especially important spawning area. Species that travel to this area to spawn include the spotfin flying fish, the Atlantic flying fish, the common two-winged and four-winged flying fish, and many others.

Scientists still have many questions about flying fish reproduction. Studies suggest, however, that different flying fish species have different spawning cycles. Flying fish of some species seem to have just one brief spawning period during their lifetimes. Other species seem to have two spawning seasons per year or perhaps one long season that continues throughout the late spring and summer months. The four-winged flying fish of the tropical Atlantic Ocean is one species that may have an extra-long spawning cycle.

Laying Eggs

As spawning season approaches, female flying fish start to develop eggs inside their bodies. A single female may carry thousands of eggs. When the time is right, she releases these eggs into the water. At the same time, males release sperm, which fertilizes the eggs. After fertilization takes place, a tiny embryo begins to form and grow inside each egg.

Flying fish eggs are round and very small, measuring less than one-tenth of an inch (2.5 millimeters) from side to side. They are heavier than water, so they tend to sink. This could be a problem in the open ocean, where the seafloor lies far below the sunny waters the eggs need for survival. But nature

The hairs on these Sargassum flying fish eggs get tangled in floating debris to keep the eggs from sinking.

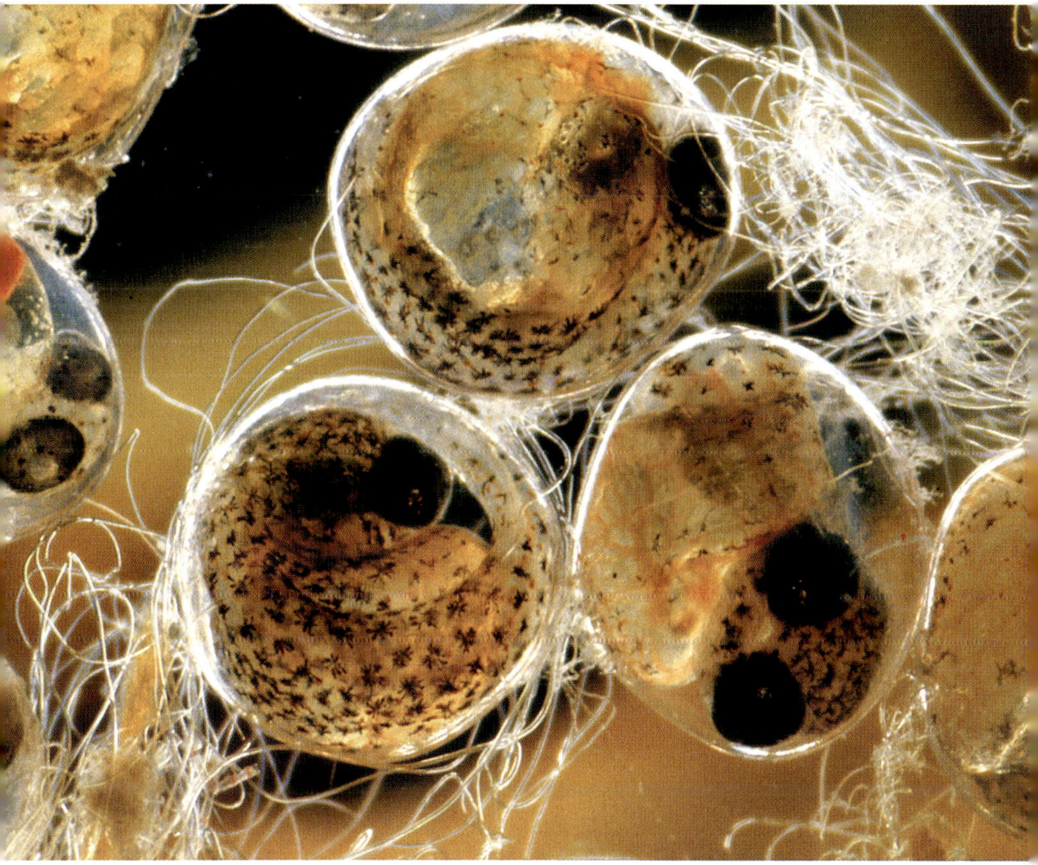

has found a way around this problem. Flying fish eggs are covered with slender hairs that may be as much as one-half inch (1.2 centimeters) long. These hairs get tangled in seaweed, bird feathers, and other floating debris, keeping the eggs from sinking. In the Sargasso Sea, some flying fish even make threads that they wrap around pieces of seaweed to form solid, floating balls. Then the fish attach hundreds of eggs to these objects to create a sort of spawning raft.

In shallow coastal waters, sinking is not such a problem for flying fish eggs. Plenty of sunlight reaches the seafloor in these areas, so the eggs have everything they need to survive no matter where they end up. After a shallow spawn, millions of fertilized eggs drop to the bottom and get stuck to rocks, coral, and other underwater objects. The eggs will cling to these objects until they are ready to hatch.

Young Fish Emerge

Hatching occurs when the flying fish embryos inside are fully developed. The mature eggs break open, releasing young fish (called **fry**) into the water. The fry are very small, measuring just one-eighth to one-quarter inch (three to six millimeters) in length. But these little animals already have all the tools they need to survive. Immediately after hatching, the tiny fish strike out on their own. They

The fins of this young four-winged flying fish are still in the developmental stage.

will make their way in the world without ever meeting their parents.

Young flying fish look very different from adults. Their heads are much broader than their bodies, and their trunks are not sleek and streamlined like

The last fins of the flying fish to develop are the large pectoral fins that give the fish its name.

those of adult flying fish. Also, a young flying fish's fins are not fully developed. All of the fins go through a growth spurt after hatching. The caudal, dorsal, and anal fins reach their adult form first, followed by the pelvic fins. Last to develop are the large, birdlike pectoral fins that give the flying fish its name.

Because flying fish fry are tiny and helpless, there is not much they can do to protect themselves from predators. But the fry of many species have built-in features that help to keep them safe. In the Sargasso Sea, for instance, most fry are brown to match the floating seaweed that surrounds them. This **camouflage** makes the young fish very hard to see. The fry do not develop their adult colors until they leave their seaweed home and start to live in the open ocean.

Young flying fish in other areas may be protected by their oddly shaped bodies. The fry of some species, for example, look like the blossoms of a certain tropical plant. This disguise keeps the fish from being eaten by hungry predators. And the fry of many other species have fleshy objects called **barbels** hanging from their heads. The barbels help to break up the fishes' body shape, which makes the animals hard to recognize and therefore less likely to be eaten. As the little flying fish get bigger, the barbels shrink. By the time the fry are fully grown, the barbels have disappeared.

Early Life

After a flying fish hatches, it becomes part of the plankton, which is a layer of tiny plants and animals floating near the ocean's surface. Tiny squid, sea stars, eels, jellyfish, and countless other creatures may be found within this population. In some parts of the ocean, the plankton contains a balanced variety of animals. In other regions, certain animals are much more plentiful than others. Because flying fish lay enormous numbers of eggs around tropical islands, flying fish fry sometimes make up a large percentage of the plankton in these areas.

Within the plankton, flying fish fry eat whatever food they can find and catch. At the same time, they try to avoid being eaten by other hungry creatures. Many young flying fish fall prey to other animals in the first few hours or days of their lives. But some get lucky. They do not run into any dangerous animals, and they find plenty of food to eat. They get bigger and stronger each day. Before long they are ready to leave the plankton and start their adult lives.

At this point, young flying fish start to gather in schools with other fry that hatched around the same time. The schools may stay near their hatching area for a few weeks. Soon, however, the flying fish are ready to explore new areas. They head out toward the open ocean, neighboring islands, or other unknown territory.

On the Move

Not much is known about the travel patterns of flying fish. Because many of these animals live far out at sea, they are hard to follow. But scientists have been able to study some species that live close to land. Scientists have discovered, for example, that Atlantic four-winged flying fish move freely be-

Its fins spread wide, this Sargassum flying fish looks ready to glide through the air above the ocean surface.

tween islands in the eastern Caribbean, while members of the same species that hatch near Brazil and some other areas do not seem to travel far from home. Varying ocean currents and other geographic factors may cause these differences in behavior. It is likely that the movements of flying fish in other parts of the world are similarly affected by local conditions.

In a global sense, though, most flying fish probably do not move far from their hatching grounds. A short life span combined with the need to return to certain spawning areas keeps these animals fairly close to home. A flying fish may roam the seas for a short part of its life, but when breeding season approaches, the fish will go wherever it must to produce young flying fish of its own. In this way new generations are produced each year, and the cycle of life continues.

chapter 3

Food on the Wing

Like all animals, flying fish must eat to survive. Flying fish fry eat mostly zooplankton (tiny animals within the plankton). Adult flying fish eat zooplankton as well but will also eat small crustaceans such as shrimp and krill. They will feed on smaller fish, too, if they get the chance. A few types of flying fish are **herbivores**, eating algae and other plants instead of animals.

But flying fish are not just hunters. Because they occur in such huge numbers, they are also important prey for many other animals. In response to this threat, flying fish have developed one of nature's most amazing defenses. They have the ability to leave the water and soar through the air to escape from predators. This ability not only gives flying fish their name, it also helps them to survive in the dangerous ocean community.

The nickname "flying fish" is actually a bit misleading. The word *flight* implies that an animal is flapping its wings to create power while in the air. This is not the case with the flying fish, which simply launches itself from the water and then glides forward on outstretched fins. But in the flying fish's case, the difference between flying and gliding is

The ability to leap out of the water and soar through the air helps flying fish escape from predators.

not important. What *is* important is staying safe, and flying fish have many tools for doing that.

Many Enemies

Flying fish have many enemies. Because these fish live so close to the sea surface, they may be eaten both by underwater animals and by creatures that live out of the water. Swimming predators include large fish such as marlins, tuna, and dorado, as well as dolphins and some other marine mammals. Open-air predators are mostly seabirds, including terns and albatrosses.

People also prey upon flying fish. These animals may be caught and used as bait for larger fish, or they may be taken for human consumption. Flying fish and their eggs are delicacies in many parts of the world, including China, Japan, and the Caribbean. As a result, many countries—especially those in the tropics—have industries devoted to the capture and sale of flying fish. Commercial fishing industries use set nets (long net walls that are anchored to the ocean floor) to snag these animals. Smaller operators that do not use set nets usually hunt for flying fish at night. Flying fish are strongly attracted to light and sometimes jump right into brightly lit fishing boats.

Staying Alive

Because flying fish are hunted by so many animals, nature has given them some built-in defenses.

A flying fish falls prey to a hungry seabird off the coast of the island of Taiwan.

Coloration is one such defense. Flying fish's bodies are **countershaded**, which means darker on top and lighter on the bottom. Seen from above, the flying fish disappears against the dark ocean depths. Seen from below, the flying fish blends into the sunny ocean surface. As a result, predators both above and below the waterline may have a hard time seeing their prey.

Schooling is another defense against predators. A hungry animal chasing a school of flying fish has thousands of possible targets, so the chances of any particular fish being caught are very small. Some fish may be eaten during an attack, but most will live to see another day.

Flying fish also use their sharp senses to spot danger. A flying fish looks around with its big eyes

Fishermen off the coast of Barbados haul in a net of flying fish, which are eaten or used as bait.

as it swims. It can also detect predators in the water below with a special organ called the **lateral line**. This organ, which runs along the flying fish's belly, senses water currents and movements. It sends information about these movements to the flying fish's brain, which reads the information and forms a picture of the fish's surroundings. If predators are nearby, chances are good that the water disturbances they make will warn flying fish of their approach.

Taking Flight

A flying fish does its best to swim away from potential predators. But sometimes a hungry animal manages to get very close before the flying fish senses it. When danger is immediate, a flying fish tries to escape by launching itself into the air and gliding away.

To prepare for flight, a flying fish folds its pectoral and pelvic fins tightly against its side to streamline its body. The fish then begins to thrash its tail back and forth. The tail is strong and creates a powerful push. Within seconds, the flying fish has reached a speed of about twenty miles per hour (thirty-two kilometers per hour).

Once the fish reaches this speed, it pokes the front part of its body out of the water at an upward angle. The fish then starts to thrash its tail even faster. The tail may beat from fifty to seventy times

Like all flying fish, this mirrorwing flying fish uses its large pectoral fins to soar above the water.

per second during this preflight phase. As the tail whips back and forth, the fish bounces across the water's surface, picking up speed with each passing instant. Before long the flying fish may be traveling as fast as forty miles per hour (sixty-four kilometers per hour). Once it is moving at top speed, the fish spreads its big pectoral fins wide and holds them rigid, like wings.

At this point, a force called **lift** comes into play. Lift is the same force that makes airplanes fly. It occurs when air flows across a wing. The air moves at different speeds above and below the wing, creating a difference in air pressure in the two places. At high speeds, the pressure above the wing can drop enough to suck an object upward. This is what happens to a fast-moving flying fish. The fish lifts off into the air, its entire body leaving the water. At this point, a two-winged flying fish depends on the lift from its pectoral fins alone. A four-winged flying fish spreads its large pelvic fins to create a bigger wing surface and thus even more lift.

In the Air

In the air, the distance a flying fish travels depends mostly on its size. Large flying fish can build up more speed before leaving the water, and they also have large wings. Large wings and high speeds create a great deal of lift, so the biggest species tend to soar the farthest. Some species can travel as much as one-eighth of a mile (0.2 kilometers) with a single jump. A big flying fish may also reach heights of 45 feet (13.7 meters) above the ocean surface. Smaller flying fish travel a much shorter distance with each leap, and they do not rise as high as their larger relatives.

A flying fish's speed drops quickly once the fish leaves the water. As the fish slows down, it falls back toward the water. But the flight is not necessarily over. If a flying fish wants to stay in the air, it positions its body so it splashes tail first into the sea. With just the long lower lobe of its caudal fin in the water, the fish starts whipping its tail back and forth again. It picks up speed as it scoots along the water's surface. Before long the fish is moving fast enough to become airborne once more.

Large species, such as this California flying fish, can glide up to one-eighth of a mile.

All flying fish have some control over their flight direction. A soaring fish can change the position of its fins to veer to the right or the left while it is in the air. Some flying fish can even make midair U-turns and fly back the way they came. These direction changes usually confuse underwater predators, which cannot tell just where their prey might land. If a flying fish is lucky, it will splash down far from any hungry animals.

A Dangerous Life

Unfortunately for flying fish, the ability to leave the water does not guarantee safety. There is always a chance that these animals will be snapped up by underwater predators when they drop back into the sea. They may also be grabbed in flight by fast-moving seabirds or caught in human fishing nets. With all the dangers of life in the ocean, many flying fish lose their lives before they reach maturity.

This high death rate is not a bad thing. Flying fish are an important food source for many ocean creatures. When they are eaten, they keep other species healthy. They escape just often enough, though, to keep their own populations strong. By "flying," these incredible creatures accomplish that goal. They also amaze people everywhere and keep up their reputation as one of the ocean's most interesting and unusual animals.

Glossary

anal fin: A fin on the bottom rear of a flying fish's body.

barbels: Fleshy objects that grow from the heads of some young flying fish.

camouflage: Coloration that helps a flying fish blend into the background.

caudal fin: Tail fin.

countershading: Body coloration that is darker on top and lighter on the bottom.

dorsal fin: A fin on the top of a flying fish's body.

embryo: Unhatched flying fish.

Exocoetidae: The scientific family name for all flying fish.

four-winged flying fish: Flying fish with large pectoral and pelvic fins.

fry: Newly hatched flying fish.

herbivore: A creature that eats only plant matter.

lateral line: An organ that detects and interprets disturbances in the water.

lift: An upward force that pulls a flying fish from the water.

pectoral fins: Side fins toward the front of a fish's body. In flying fish, the pectoral fins are large and act as wings.

pelvic fins: Side fins toward the rear of a fish's body. Some flying fish have large pelvic fins that act as wings.

spawn: To release eggs and sperm into the water.

two-winged flying fish: Flying fish with large pectoral fins and small pelvic fins.

For Further Exploration

Books

Nic Bishop, *The Secrets of Animal Flight*. Boston: Houghton Mifflin, 1997. Topics include taking off and landing, soaring and gliding, and different types of wings in the animal kingdom.

Mary M. Cerullo, *Sea Soup: Zooplankton*. Gardiner, ME: Tilbury House, 2001. Presents fabulous photos and information regarding planktonic krill, jellyfish, and the larval stages of many fish and crustaceans.

Encyclopedia of the Aquatic World. Vol. 4. New York: Marshall Cavendish, 2004. Includes an excellent overview of flying fish and their relatives.

Peter Riley, *Food Chains*. New York: Franklin Watts, 1998. Introduces the basic science behind food chains and presents experiments to show how they work.

Web Sites

Flying Fish (www.smithfieldschicken.com/html/Kids_only/flying_fish.htm). Catch the flying fish in this fun, online game.

Life in the Rainforest (www.szgdocent.org/ff/f-rain1a.htm). This page includes lots of good information about gliding animals.

Index

Picture Credits

Cover image: © Tony Arruza/CORBIS
© Tony Arruza/CORBIS, 11, 35
© Jonathan Blair/CORBIS, 15
© Richard Herrmann/Visuals Unlimited, 13
© 2002 Image Quest 3-D, 23, 25, 29
© Chris Newbert/Minden Pictures, 26
© Doug Perrine/SeaPics.com, 18, 32
© Todd Pusser/SeaPics.com, 39
© Reuters/CORBIS, 34
© Kim Taylor/Bruce Coleman Inc., 7
© Norbert Wu/Minden Pictures, 14, 37
Steve Zmina, 16, 21

About the Author

Kris Hirschmann has written more than one hundred books for children. She is the president of The Wordshop, a business that provides a variety of writing and editorial services. She holds a bachelor's degree in psychology from Dartmouth College in Hanover, New Hampshire.

Hirschmann lives just outside Orlando, Florida, with her husband, Michael, and her daughters, Nikki and Erika.